SASSAFRAS DE BRUYN has a degree in illustrative design from St. Lucas Antwerp University College of Art & Design. Her other books include *Everywhere All Around* and *Cleo* (both Clavis). Sassafras lives in Ghent, Belgium, where she is the illustrator for the Kopergietery Children's and Youth Theatre. Visit her website at sassafrasdebruyn.com.

First published in the United States in 2020
by Eerdmans Books for Young Readers,
an imprint of Wm. B. Eerdmans Publishing Co.
Grand Rapids, Michigan

www.eerdmans.com/youngreaders

Originally published in Belgium by Lannoo
www.lannoo.com

Original edition © 2018 Lannoo Publishers
Original title: *De jager en zijn hond*
Translated from the Dutch language

English-language translation © 2020 Eerdmans Books for Young Readers

Manufactured in China

29 28 27 26 25 24 23 22 21 20   1 2 3 4 5 6 7 8 9

 **FLANDERS LITERATURE** This book was published with the support of Flanders Literature

Library of Congress Cataloging-in-Publication Data

Names: De Bruyn, Sassafras, author.
Title: The hunter and his dog : a fantastical journey through the world of
    Bruegel / Sassafras De Bruyn.
Other titles: Jager en zijn hond. English.
Description: Grand Rapids, Michigan : Eerdmans Books for Young Readers,
    2020. | Originally published: Tielt, Belgium : Lannoo Publishers, 2018
    under the title, De jager en zijn hond. | Includes bibliographical
    references. | Audience: Ages 5-9 | Summary: A wordless picture book in
    which a hunter and his dog travel through a series of scenes painted by
    Pieter Bruegel the Elder. Includes a biographical sketch of Bruegel and
    information about the paintings featured.
Identifiers: LCCN 2019026846 | ISBN 9780802855343 (hardcover)
Subjects: LCSH: Bruegel, Pieter, approximately 1525-1569—Juvenile fiction.
    | CYAC: Bruegel, Pieter, approximately 1525-1569—Fiction. | Painting,
    Belgian—Fiction. | Art appreciation—Fiction.
Classification: LCC PZ7.1.B7987 Hun 2020 | DDC [E]—dc23
LC record available at https://lccn.loc.gov/2019026846

THE HUNTER AND HIS DOG

A Fantastical Journey through the World of Bruegel

SASSAFRAS DE BRUYN

Eerdmans Books for Young Readers

Grand Rapids, Michigan

ABOUT PIETER BRUEGEL AND HIS WONDERFUL WORLD

Pieter Bruegel was born around 1525, probably in what is now the Netherlands—a quiet beginning in an anything but quiet time. People had plenty to argue about in the sixteenth century: church reformers, scientific and artistic revolutions, and the rule of a distant Spanish king. In this busy, bustling world, Pieter Bruegel started creating worlds of his own.

By his twenties the young artist was studying under Pieter Coecke van Aelst, a respected painter, sculptor, architect, and designer. The apprenticeship probably also exposed him to paintings by Hieronymus Bosch (1450–1516), whose strange scenes would shape Bruegel's later creations. In 1551 Bruegel joined an artists' guild and began to paint, travel, and make sketches for a printmaker in Antwerp. But he must have missed his teacher's family—or at least, his teacher's daughter. Bruegel married Mayken Coecke in 1563, moving to Brussels to be nearer to her mother. In this new city he created many of his best-known works, including *The Hunters in the Snow* and *The Harvesters*.

Even while painting in Brussels and Antwerp, Bruegel's mind was often in the countryside. Previous artists had focused on religious scenes and situations, but Bruegel believed that there was something important—even holy—in everyday life. From the summer harvest to a country wedding, ordinary subjects were just as worthy of time, interest, and paint. Today Bruegel is considered a pioneer of peasant and landscape painting.

The painter's landscapes capture settings and seasons, allowing viewers to appreciate the world around them. *The Hunters in the Snow*, part of a series of paintings based on the twelve months, was one of the world's first paintings to embrace winter in all its harsh beauty. Each brushstroke plunges viewers into knee-deep snow and the thrill of cold air. The hunters and their dogs droop their heads and bend their knees, so exhausted from their failed hunt that they miss the rabbit tracks beside them. Though the painting shows their disappointment, it also captures the loveliness of a landscape filled with grey, blue, and white.

Bruegel's peasants, too, call viewers' attention to what they might usually ignore. One story says that Bruegel and a friend would disguise themselves as peasants and sneak into country banquets. If that's true, the artist was obviously noticing every detail! From wedding guests to playing children, the people in his paintings overflow with personality and humor. They flirt, they play leapfrog and hide-and-seek, and they lick the last of a good meal off their fingers. Their faces, their actions, and their emotions are all vividly and recognizably human.

But Bruegel knew that humans could also be cruel, foolish, and ignorant. *The Land of Cockaigne* mocks people so overindulgent that even a roof tiled with pies isn't enough food! *The Tower of Babel*, with its winding pathways and doors to nowhere, reminds viewers just how pointless pride can be. And we can also be self-absorbed, too busy with our own work to help others. In *Landscape with the Fall of Icarus*, neither a shepherd nor a fisherman nor a plowman notice that—just behind them—a man is falling from the sky.

Pieter Bruegel died of an unknown cause in 1569, and that could have been the end of his artistic legacy. But his family would continue to make art for hundreds of years to come. Mayken's mother, a skilled painter of miniatures, probably tutored her grandsons. Jan Brueghel and Pieter Brueghel the Younger painted still lifes and floral scenes, and they trained their own children in the trade. (While Bruegel the Elder dropped the *h* from his surname, his relatives and descendants called themselves Brueghels.) Over two centuries later, members of the family were still creating painted worlds.

But the artist's descendants weren't (and aren't) the only ones wishing to enter Bruegel's landscapes and scenes. Bruegel influenced painters Peter Paul Rubens and Édouard Manet, and both W.H. Auden and William Carlos Williams wrote poems after viewing *Landscape with the Fall of Icarus*. When the Kunsthistorisches Museum in Vienna hosted an exhibition of Bruegel's work in 2018 and 2019, half a million people visited in less than four months. And when scientists started naming Mercury's craters, one of them received a familiar name: Bruegel.

In his time and ours, Bruegel's paintings welcome viewers into an extraordinary world. Every little detail reminds us to stop, look, and look again.

Netherlandish Proverbs (1559)

Gemäldegalerie, Berlin

The Fight between Carnival and Lent (1559)

Kunsthistorisches Museum, Vienna

Children's Games (1560)

Kunsthistorisches Museum, Vienna

The Fall of the Rebel Angels (1562)
Royal Museums of Fine Arts of Belgium, Brussels

Dulle Griet (1563)
Museum Mayer van den Bergh, Antwerp

The Triumph of Death (1562)
Museo del Prado, Madrid

The Tower of Babel (1563)
Kunsthistorisches Museum, Vienna

The Peasant Dance (1568)
Kunsthistorisches Museum, Vienna

The Wedding Dance (1566)
Detroit Institute of Arts, Detroit

The Peasant Wedding (1567)
Kunsthistorisches Museum, Vienna

Landscape with the Fall of Icarus (1558)
Royal Museums of Fine Arts of Belgium, Brussels (copy)

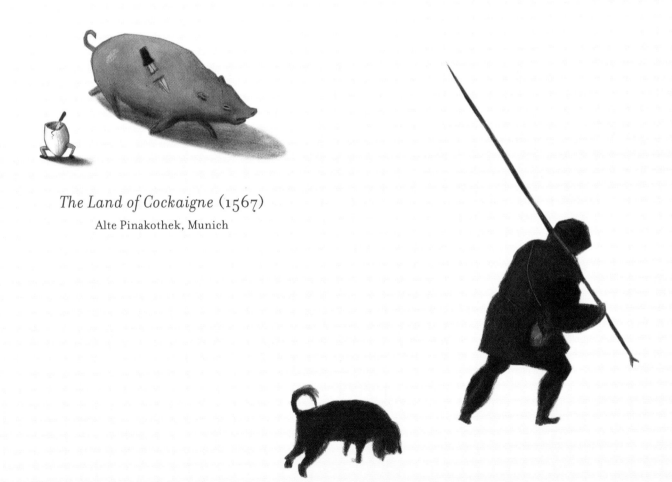

The Land of Cockaigne (1567)
Alte Pinakothek, Munich

The Hunters in the Snow (1565)
Kunsthistorisches Museum, Vienna

MORE ON BRUEGEL

BOOKS

Ddang, Haneul. *The People in the Paintings: The Art of Bruegel*. Illus. Jae-seon Ahn. Strathfield, Australia: Big & Small, 2017.
Bruegel's peasants and children guide readers through the details of his paintings.

Kérillis, Hélène. *A Bird in Winter: A Children's Book Inspired by Pieter Bruegel the Elder*. Illus. Stéphane Girel. New York: Prestel Publishing, 2011.
In this picture book set within *The Hunters in the Snow*, eight-year-old Mayken nurses a bird back to health.

Mühlberger, Richard. *What Makes a Bruegel a Bruegel?* New York: Viking, 1993.
Painting by painting, this book helps readers understand Bruegel's passion for peasants and landscapes.

Venezia, Mike. *Getting to Know the World's Greatest Artists: Pieter Bruegel*. New York: Children's Press, 1993.
Illustrated with comics, this biography introduces children to Bruegel's life and work.

ONLINE AND VIDEO

British Broadcasting Corporation, *BBC Tales of Winter: The Art of Snow and Ice*.
This documentary highlights *The Hunters in the Snow* and its impact on artists' perceptions of winter beauty.

Google Arts & Culture, *Pieter Bruegel*.
Google's immersive gathering of Bruegel material includes explanations of the paintings, a timeline of his work, and links to related artists and movements.

Kunsthistorisches Museum, *Inside Bruegel*.
Visitors can explore the Bruegel paintings from the museum's collection, including *The Tower of Babel* and *The Peasant Wedding*, through macrophotography, infrared macrophotography, infrared reflectography, and X-radiography. The website also records the museum's restoration efforts.